Where's the Bear?
pictures by Byron Barton
words by Charlotte Pomerantz
Greenwillow Books, New York

Library of Congress Cataloging in Publication Data   Pomerantz, Charlotte.   Where's the bear? Summary: A group of townspeople go looking for a bear.   [1. Bears—Fiction.   2. Stories in rhyme.   I. Barton, Byron, ill.   II. Title.   PZ8.3.P564Wh   1983   [E]   83-1697   ISBN 0-688-01752-5 ISBN 0-688-01753-3 (lib. bdg.)

For Louise and Aaron

Where's the bear?

Where's the bear?

Where?

There's the bear. There's the bear.

There's the bear.

There.

Where's the bear? There's the bear.

Where's the bear?

There's the bear.

There's the bear.

There's the bear.